NORTHWOOD

NORTHWOOD

Maryse Meijer

BLACK
BALLOON
PUBLISHING

Copyright © 2018 by Maryse Meijer
First published in the United States in 2018 by Black Balloon,
an imprint of Catapult (catapult.co)

Jacket and book design by Jonathan Yamakami
Jacket illustrations by Rufus Newell

ISBN: 978-1-948226-01-1

Catapult titles are distributed to the trade
by Publishers Group West
Phone: 866-400-5351

Library of Congress Control Number: 2018938765

Printed in China
10 9 8 7 6 5 4 3 2 1

For D.

Because

a fire

THE WORLD

I don't draw you anymore.

I want

       to see

            through the trees.

               The way the pen   used

                                   to feel,

a weapon,   drawing   blood   from the page:

                not a hymn,

       not   an homage—

    why are the best songs   love songs   I want

to draw

       , death but   death   doesn't   make

       music. On the page   or

            elsewhere.

                         The wood

doesn't care   if you live

                         or die.   It

is dying   all the time. Living.   Unsurprised.

But I

              am not

                  a wood, I am not   a stream I mourn

                                      the branch that

                  breaks   from its body

and I want

to make   a mark   more than I want

                                      to make   love

but I was

                  only

              ever   good   at   this one

                                      fucking   thing

THE HIEROPHANT

I'd only been away
for a day no city no

sky I recognized, how full it was,
the hard stars so cold-shouldered

blinking *You are alone,*
Only not quite:

there was the stream, after all, and the trees,
and ants relentless over the counters,

the foxes fucking their way through the evenings
their screams so human it chilled me,
    high slaughterhouse sound

whistling in every direction.

I could not get the fire started and the floors had no carpets
and the boots I brought had a hole in them and the dew
    came through.

I went out to the porch and put my head against the post.
I knew what a car was. I knew

convenience stores and dollar hot dogs and coffee
    that appeared
when my money appeared and the phone ready to ring
    and the traffic like the sea

lapping the concrete coast of the sidewalk,
24 hours, something always open.

I wanted to get away and I was away
and there was that sky that seemed to say, *You know nothing.*

I took my pencils out, my paper, my ink.
The rough table was short on one leg and when I drew

it rocked from one side to the other.
Moths flew from the cabinets.

I had never been in love.

KINDLING

I saw the light on in the woodcutter's hut and walked
through the leaves and knocked on his door not knowing
he was there on the porch sitting in the dark a blanket
across his lap he said What. I said I'm alone I can't start the
fire. My nose dripped. I had no gloves. I thought it would be
warm, my first month in the woods. I just stood there. He got
up and I followed him into the cabin, my cabin, and he took
the box of long matches from the mantel and showed me.
How dry the wood had to be. Stacked just so. Blow. Smoke
in my eyes. How it stung. Squatting side by side I sniffed the
cold coming off him how long did he sit outside like that in
the dark it was so dark. The fire swelled, After a moment he
left. Sparkle.

Snap.

And the burn

ORBIT

I'll speak just once, here,
about my father.

You were nothing like him:
he was small, lean as a young tree

and scared. He sat in corners
and cleaned his glasses

and tried to smile. He was almost never
there. I mean in his head he wasn't.

He liked to see me
with my pens, at the kitchen table:

he said I would be
a great artist

though he was an insurance man
who couldn't name a single painting.

He told me
before he disappeared

about the way he thought
I should love.

Don't marry, he said,
the one you like best.

That's the way to keep it, you know.
Friction

slows a thing down.
Love him

from a distance. And he'll always
be yours.

I said, Yes Dad.
I was ten and uncomprehending.

A year later he left the house
with his pipe and his favorite

shirt
and was found

hanging in a garage
two states away.

I wonder whose heart
he didn't dare hold close.

I mean,
other than mine

THE DANCE HALL

I knew no one. A bar at the edge of the wood and music I hadn't heard music in a week or seen a human face and there was yours, a miracle, selling tickets at the door; you took my hand and stamped it black. Jade eyes into mine and silver hair, older than any man I'd ever thought was beautiful, your beauty the first thing that hurt and I moved into the room solid with plaid shirts and me in my black dress so this is the country. I drank a cup of punch and ate almonds from a plastic bowl and you came and dug your hand next to mine wiped your salty fingers on your hip and looked down at my shirt unironed and crooked teeth agleam in the yellow light. I didn't spend a minute saying no. You led me through the music, under your arm, pressed against your side, sweat slicking us wherever we touched. I spun and you stopped me and said *Where are you staying*. I saw the ring on your finger. The bottom dropping out. We talked on the stage steps, half hidden by a ficus. A cup of punch on your knee, jeans so tight at the thigh I could see how big you were. I blushed, touched it anyway. Not a sound from you. Watching my face, little smile, devastation: the music grew. *Where's your wife*, I said, and you laughed: we would never be in public together again. *I think I'm drunk*, I said, moving my hand away. *There's no booze in that punch, darling*, you said, and got me another glass.

ASCALON

St. George—
helmet aslant, boot on the back.

But where is victory?
The staff never moves,

hovers just above the tongue.
He'll wait forever for that hard kiss.

I make a list: spear, spurs,
silver, speed.

Good luck, George says.
And the dragon

winks.

FIRST

Slapped between the sheets no ceremony you skinned me
stockings to boots I hadn't shaved I couldn't spread my legs
you got in anyway. No condom no question *Did you want* or
Have you got just your hand against my face, a stroke before
the slap. I was dry when you got inside. I hid from you. I
didn't come. Your skin in my mouth, bitter, delicious, you too
close to see, what was touching me, your breath all around,
the sound of something chasing us. It caught up.

AMATEUR

I drew my way through the year, having dropped out of
everything. That ad for the cabin written for someone like
me, who didn't know what *Get Away Cheap* meant; you can't
get away. I went to live like a nun, pure, distractionless.
One packed bag. I wanted to draw nature. Tired of drawing
people. Instead I drew you: as a tree, a fox, a stream, a dragon,
a devil. I drew you as I used to draw myself, at first to make
more of you, later to get rid of you, and now I don't draw you
at all, there are other things, and I never got it right.

ADONIS

We met once
two towns over

for breakfast. A diner. Butter
sunk in the muffins. Two plates

of bacon. There was snow
stuck to the windows, a waitress

in blue pulling at her stocking.
We sat on the same side

in a booth and I held your hand so tight.
How strange to have you

out in the world. Coffee. Syrup.
the way you liked your eggs

gutted on toast.

What, you said, your mouth full,
I kept touching

your face. You brought it closer

to mine, looked in my eyes. There was some
promise there. Some bargain. A roach

on the floor. Just let me look at you.
The check came. We left

in separate cars.

ELEGY

For a while in the wood I was drawing scissors. Before the
dance, before your hands, I didn't even have a premonition
of you, no black mark against the moon, no bad dream
folded into the sheet, it was just me, and that old table, and
my model, lying in my lap. I'd found them in a drawer of
useless things—snapped rubber bands, birthday candles,
half a package of yellowed paper plates. Silver blades, brass
handle, I tested the tips against the side of my finger—oh,
they could cut, those scissors, but not there, no, you couldn't
chop a tree with them, or make a path; the wood wanted
harder things, a knife, an ax. When I found a loose thread on
my shirt I didn't think of the scissors, her legs spread on the
table beside the bed: I just put the hem to my lips and bit.

INTAGLIO

The striped mattress, how thin it was, the wire cot beneath
biting into my bones the blankets

folded double did not help.
I don't know what makes a person willing.

One evening I ran out of ink
and that same evening you brought me three new jars

and we sat testing them to see
if the different colors had different smells

or if black was really distinguishable
via a faint taste of licorice. We laughed like pigs.

Showing each other our colored tongues.
You put your head on my shoulder

and knocked a drop of ink on the mattress,
    where it bloomed
and darkened

and dried. I got quiet, watching it.
What, you said.

I shook my head.
I had stripped myself of every other longing,
    of every possible

human comfort but in that moment, eating poison
    from the jars,
how wealthy I was, how fragile, how strong, like the strange

skin of a bubble that can resist so much and then
nothing at all.

I watched my happiness sink through the unmade bed
where the blanket had been pushed aside,

one stain among many.
Open your mouth, you said,

and I did,
but it was too late, and the mattress was dry.

I drove   looking   for your house

                    license plate   memorized

dead   lawn   No flags   for you no

lashing the   bushes   you had   money.

couldn't take me.   Miles of   trees   I

the same   mailbox   out of   gas.

filled me   up   I   could

          the pictures.   Your

          licking   the   screen   the endless green

spread   wide   and the only   truly cruel thing

                                        Darling,

your car white   I had never been   inside

        it's not   this   driveway   this

cheap   holiday   decoration

Lots   of land   somewhere   my car

     cried   after three hours   circling

     Someone   came by   with a can

have   fucked him/   didn't.   I saw

     back   door.   The dog

        of your kingdom   your arms

     you ever said

            you will never find it.

MOTHER

It's Christmas.
I know.
You have something to cook on there?
Mom.
What are you going to eat?
I'll go out.
Where? There's nothing there, I looked.
Looked where?
Google maps.
You're crazy.
Me?
Well I just can't make it, I'm sorry.
(quiet) *Are you drawing?*
Yes.
That's something, at least.
At least.
I don't mean it that way.
It's good for me.
(pause) *Is there—*
I've got to go. This thing cuts out all the time.
And I'm running out—
—a man?
—of minutes. No.
What are the people like?
Like people.
Do you need money?
Yes but don't send it.
What do you mean don't send it?
I don't want anything.
You sound strange.
It's the phone.

The phone?
Because I hate talking on it and then I say things.
Are you sure—
It's work. I'm working.
You can tell me—
Mom.
You'll starve.
(silence)
Are there bears?
(sigh)
Because honey I know you

you'd let one eat you right up—

NIGHT SONG

You brought batteries for the radio.
We danced close, the way we couldn't at the dance hall,

your cock against my thigh.
We danced those batteries out.

I took them, spent, when I left,

Bobby Hatfield's sad falsetto
ringing through the copper caps.

Candles quivering against the glass, our shadows
hovering above our heads I will never forget

the spider's egg opening in the corner, her babies
spilling across the wall as you dug your chin into my neck.

Walking through song after song.

The thing is, you were soft.
The white of a barely cooked egg, the glistening

edge of it, how it trembles on metal.
You kept falling in love.

The spiders
found the cracks, made new nests. They ate

the ants. And the radio sat on the shelf
above the little blackened pan with its scrawny omelets

and said nothing.

DAPHNE

Her back against   me   catching her

        deep breaths.   Naked she was   smooth   as pith

hair   caught   in a branch I pulled   it free.

The women   kneel   at the root   I watch.

How determined they are   to bleed.   Apollo's gold eyes

didn't dazzle me I

prefer   the stream   she opens her book and   learns her trees

    the flies   are heavy this time   of year she

        combs them from her

bangs   at night   she's thinking   more and more

        how to

    escape it   should she   escape

where's your daddy I asked

isn't he   a god

CELL

It worked
sometimes. Blue light in the dark
and your name in black
on the screen hardly ever
showing up. You didn't need
to call: when you came
I was here.
Every time. Unerring this sense
of pussy and where
to find it.
Strung up in the smokehouse or waiting their turn beneath
    the ice—
you know where the bodies are.
You put them there.

SHOPPING LIST

In the market fingering a box of tea I heard you laugh
two aisles over. My hand froze on the plastic; there was a
woman's voice, laughing with you. I pressed against the
metal shelf, coat buttons tapping the cereal boxes below.
Who knew me here, I wondered, was I still a stranger, a
woman shivering against the Liptons? On the edge of the
wood it was especially dangerous: the one road with its strip
of shops, the bar, the dance hall, the gas station, the Feed
and Seed. Humans. I closed my eyes and heard your heavy
stride. The breeze your body makes so close to mine. You
didn't slow. I had eight dollars in change and a hole in my
jeans and a fraction of a lover and I felt it, my poverty, how
little I knew, the limits

FREEDOM

Fourth of July barbecue balancing a plate of cake on my knees my mother said Remember that time you went to live in that old cabin? Laughing in fresh disbelief I never did understand why you did that. The mosquitoes whined in my ear, chewed their way through my ankles. I looked at a girl in the next yard holding a sparkler against the sky; the smell of gunpowder, the lethal taste of vodka lemonade. I didn't say a thing. Don't you? my mother said. Remember? How weird you were on the phone and then coming back to gain all that weight? The cake slid off the plate, and the dogs lapped it up. I was walking to the back door. How cold the empty kitchen was. I was actively not remembering. There were no parades, in the woods. No firecrackers no dogs no mothers no refrigerator hum no beers on ice just my hair gathered in his hands and my back bent in the firelight that was the time he got in up to the wrist and I stopped breathing. A stranger in the woods whistling The Star-Spangled Banner as he passed the window we were both amazed there was not a single drop of blood when it was over but you're in the kitchen you had too much to drink you were there and now you're here deep breath see? There's your husband now, asking you if there's an extra jar of hot sauce somewhere he can't find it. You can find it, go outside with him, put the jar on the grill, the sun slapping your face afresh, that girl still wasting sparklers before it's even dark the green light spitting off into nothing and look, your mother has another piece of cake, and a fork, and you'll eat a bite of it, just a bite, and you'll say how good it is, because it is good, you made it yourself.

HOOD

You glued together a broken dish. I sat sewing a hole
on your cuff. The rain

tapped down the chimney
smoked

the fire we were trying out
a new kind of

cracker.
A slice of cheese

on the knife. This domestic scene,
new to me, precious, it could have been

the Fifties. Until
your phone

lights up. You stare at the screen.
Damn, you say. *Damn, damn.*

I freeze. Choke
on a seed

and sleep
for a hundred years.

By midday the wood
is empty of princes and the sink

is streaked with bile.
I'll never eat

that cheese again,
or thread that dull needle, touch

the jar of glue.

Many nights later you come,
tapping at the glass,

a wolf in wolves' clothing: what time is it?
What day?

Shh, you say, *sh sh*.
Strike a match.

Haven't you cleaned? you wonder.
A beetle in the kettle. It reeks in here.

I reach for your belt.
Making my own coffin.

THE FOOL

The woodcutter saw the marks on my face, heard me
scream when you said you would not come for a week,
saw you through the window pushing me against the wall,
just hard enough to rattle the glass, your arm against my
throat and you saying Stop. Just like in bed but different,
I didn't scream, then, no one could hear you fucking me,
that was the rule, my favorite rule, I relished it, that silence;
now it chokes me. Your face close enough for me to see the
red thread in your eyes, the gray lines in your teeth: Just
be quiet, you hissed. The room blacked out behind you. I
was shrunk to the size of your thumb. When you let me go
I rolled along the wall, coughing; I saw him, on the path,
looking in, no expression; your hands shaking on your
keys. The fire spat a cinder onto the rug and you crushed it
beneath your boot. My head on the thick leather laces. How
did he know you weren't killing me? Did I know? Did you?
Cradling the back of my neck you said Darling, get up, and I
stood. Saw the long drop down. Stepped into air

PATH

if I could have seen the forest for the trees
if I could have seen the forest from afar and stayed afar
if I could have known how deep the woods went
if I could have gone less quickly
if I could have gone less deeply, if I could have gone less
if I could have known the danger
if I could have heeded what I did know, that I was the danger
       making danger
if I could have held on to something other than your silk side
if I could have kept my hands from seeking that silk so often
if I could stop all this salt
if I could stop seeing these trees
if I could stop the branches of these trees, stop their budding,
       their shedding,
   their dying, their deaths
   how they astound me
if I could see just one more bloom of you
if I could keep a single seed

EMPRESS

Get up, you said. I didn't. I felt like something pink sinking
to the bottom of a very deep sea. Your shirt on the floor. I
plucked the empty sleeve. Witless. Where was I? Oh yes.
Here. Your beautiful legs. You touched my hair. I spat. It's
tradition, after all: one in a long long line. Next time I might
like lipstick, mints. The blackbirds tapped the glass. A chain
saw roared. You pulled me up by the elbow; I hit my knee on
the chair. I ate dinner without washing, skin stiff, a spot on
my shirt. Blue beneath my cheek.

I don't know anymore. I never did. You smiled across the
table and I remembered something else I could do with this
thing: smile back.

PERSPECTIVE

I could diminish you.
Itemize the missing tooth,

the careless clothes,
every time you couldn't get it up.

The way your age betrayed you.

But why should I make you smaller than you were.
Than you are.

In truth, you look the same from here
as you did from there—

Immortal. Pristine.

SMALL TOWN

I flipped through the plastic sleeve of photos—there were
your children, I didn't want them at all—but the wife, yes,
let's take a look. Very cold I said *Well she's quite a lot older
than me. Yes*, you said, careful not to be offended, careful,
sometimes, with me, in this way, as if holding a very full
glass of acid. After a while I said *She's pretty* in a deflated
voice and you looked at the picture and said *Yes* again. Like
you regretted it. *What are we doing here* I said, and you
shrugged, put your hands in your pocket along with the
wallet *Being together*. Which was true, there in the wood
I was being, moment to moment, as I was nowhere else
before or since. There was a knock at the door. I thought,
breathless, *Her*. But you went to the door shirtless saying
Yes? And I hid my face in the blanket. *That your car?* the
woodcutter said. *It's on my lot. Sorry*, you said, *I'm going
in a moment*. He knew you. He knew your wife, too. You
shrugged: small town.

THE WOODCUTTER

His is the hut that butts the clearing.
I spied him tanning hides, stretching skins.

He had your exact width of thumb.
What is the rule for whipping, I inquired; he said

Ask your man. I asked.
Belt and bruise and rose and gold.

And then you withdrew to the window,

your back to me.
What I read there I will never write,

nor will I even think it,
your shoulders sloped just so.

⸰

Branch over branch: this is where

it grows thickest.
This is where I crawled in small

and then grew big and could not
come out again.

The hatchet man came and did his chopping,
not caring if he clipped a finger, or a face.

Most maids must have terror
before they get their prince.

The queens suffer, too.
Not to mention the kids,

the burning witch, the wolves and the wild
pigs, anything with wings. Where

did the bread go?
Or didn't we bring any,

thinking we were too much home
to make a trail?

°

Now I am on my stomach by the stream,
whispering into the water. I think this is where

we drank. I think this is where
the woodcutter came, and took me by my hair,

and made me lick stone.
His eyes were not unlike your eyes. I felt the old wounds open.

I smirched the stream.

°

Are you listening?
I can hear his boots in the bower.

ENEMY

When you caught your breath you smiled. Sorry you said I'm
sorry, tracing circles on my stomach. You talked in a normal
voice about something I didn't hear and then you looked up
after a while and said Oh are you crying?

PLAGUE

It came up beneath the sheet. I didn't scream seized the hot
body brought it to my face nose to nose my hand around
its neck. If there were easier or better ways to kill a rat I did
not know them, I was in bed after all. My fingers almost met
through the flesh of its throat half asleep I was squeezing it
like a piece of fruit some enormous fury floating above us. It
wasn't easy, I realized, to not stop yourself. That little body
beneath me, treading the air please don't, please don't. Too
late I let it go. Belly slack. Its eye turned to stone.

FEAST

And yet this is where we fuck—
the mold blooming in the bath
the towel in my mouth
your come a yellow flower on the water,
my blood jeweling my thigh.
I wipe up what I can.
You open the window.
The birds eat from my hands.

HEDERA

We'll tell you   something

                                                        about that

woodcutter he

        isn't   so clear   a custodian

        as you think he

lets us grow   up   the glass he hates

                    the light   on the

TV screen   turning the picture   white

    there was

        a daughter   once.

A red-haired thing he   called   Creusa.

        You see he was

as fond of myths   as you.   Listen that girl

left her father   to rot   and you   don't look   anything like her yet

he hates   you   still.   Don't let the rumor   soften you

pity

has no place   here   if something

is growing

and it   pleases   you

let it grow   if not   rip it   right   out

but

he has let you, too,   fill up   the windows he   wants   to see

what   you'll   do.

Stick

or sink.

Grow feet   for the glass.

Take   the ax.

Or it will take you.

BREAK

When I told you about the rat you thought I'd gone crazy.
Darling there are traps, you said; anyway, they don't want
anything in here, you take a broom, you shoo it outside.
It's mice you have to worry about. I showed you my hands,
the palms scrubbed raw. What's wrong with you? you said,
the crawling sensation still in my skin, I couldn't get rid of
it, couldn't touch food, hadn't eaten all day, it died right
there. You stroked and stroked the sting, making it worse,
it was hurting, you couldn't stop. I was stuttering into your
shoulder. You got inside me still holding my hands, kissing
through the snot, little murderess, little death-dealer, you
couldn't help it, none of us ever could.

GROVE

I sat on your lap you laid your head against my back saying
into my spine *I understand, I don't know why I pretended I
didn't. I understand everything you do.* And you believed it.
That you understood. Why the trees were twisted, why some
grew in air or hobbled alone across the white page, leafless,
dripping. You'd accused me of insisting on desolation and I
said, no, no, this is what it means to be a tree, a tree is alone,
it lives long past everything else that could know it. I don't
mean to make the tree small; it is we who are small. That's
what I meant. I never drew myself next to you. It was you
alone, the tree alone. Me beyond the branch, a gleaming.

CUPID

It is   the   immortal

        a hot   white   wave

a   monster

stirring   the water.

It takes no   delight   in what   it does.

It just

            does.

NARCISSUS

When it was warmer we rolled our pants to our knees and
stepped through the stream. Good old ice water, an ache
deep in the flesh, I followed you over the moss. We talked
calmly about the end of my lease on the cottage, walking
against the current, me in the *V* left by your legs, my eyes on
the rocks, on you, on the rocks. What, here, could love me?
Not you, climbing the ladder of fallen logs with easy steps,
leaving me at the bottom, foot caught between stones. You
were too high up to take my hand, though you reached for
me anyway: *Come on.* To get free I skinned myself from
ankle to toe and there was blood in the water, a sullen swirl,
staining your face in the stream.

LINEAGE

Here's my face, you say/ my breast/ the wet/ secret/ he never
really left/ a mark./ That's how good/ he was/ and you are
proud/ of how you took it/ the star/ the tragic/ lead/ you are
a giver./ Of head/ of silences./ It's not really/ separable./
His pleasure/ eventually/ your pleasure/ the solar plexus/
punched windless/ sometimes he simply/ beat the crap
out of you/ and it became/ sex?/ I'm asking you/ what you
make of that/ kind of/ penetration/ how it makes/ all the
other kinds/ less simple/ or was it ever/ simple/ even when
you are alone/ in the dark/ and you come/ just thinking of
your blood/ on his hand/

TEMPERANCE

The blackness.
Side by side.
Hunger pains and then

nothing. The still hours,
when love sets like crystal,
heart hard with it.

Some swollen cloud.
Windless sky.
Your leg across mine,

keeping me lame. No reason to move again,
not even to reach for the cup,
its smooth skin of poison.

That cloud, suddenly vanished.
The beetles with their tiny jaws,
eating the last of our backs.

PRIESTESS

Your mistress strutted about the Sunday market with a
green string bag and espadrilles, as old as my mother but
sleeker, bare arms like marble, breasts as high and full as
the baskets before her. I stood at a table of potatoes and
thrust my hand into the parsley and thought very hard
about how often you went to bed with her, how often with
me, how good you were at minutes, putting them in their
proper slots. It was spring and I had a pair of sunglasses
on and the same filthy jacket I'd worn all winter the sun
was crawling over the backs of my hands I could hear those
espadrilles grinding into the gravel how I wanted to tell
her Look. Just two weeks more would it kill you to give
them to me I won't ever come back. She was filling that
bag up just pointing to everything and it was given to her
and she laughed and I crumpled an onion skin in my fist
she didn't have the sense to look my way, to see how much
more beautiful I was and so I looked at the man selling the
potatoes and said too loud *How much?* He pointed to a sign.
The onion skin dissolved. My bag was empty. She turned
and our eyes met across the throng and we waved.

TECHNICAL TERM FOR HEARTBREAK

Fall was my first season and my last. I didn't like the way the
leaves got wet in the rain and stuck to my boots made me
slip long scrape on my hip bruised all around. A thin calm
spread through me; I think that's how you know you're going
to lose your mind.

There was one night you came, a night that would turn into a
morning and then an afternoon, sixteen or seventeen hours,
a miracle, and yet mostly what we did was sleep. We arose no
rush in the morning brushing our teeth before kissing and
later I thought, what incomprehensible stupidity, waste, I
wept over it, I hit my head with my fist, why? Why did I?

It did not save me any grief to go numb at the sound of your
car, arriving. It did not drain the pus from the panic when
I heard you leave, for the final time, the tires on the leaves
and then the sound of the dirt and rubber over stone I heard
everything, you know, I went to the door and died.

THE HERMIT

I took the blanket, the batteries, the cups. The notebooks,
the empty ink jars, the novels you'd given me, a picture
I pinched from your wallet. I left our hair in the bath. I
stripped the bed, drove with the sheets in my lap, didn't cry
at the traffic lights, cried in the travel plaza over a plate of
cold fries. Like in the movies I cut my hair in the bathroom
as soon as I got home. I put the sheets on the bed in the city
and I smelled us in them and didn't wash. The noise outside
my door made me cry. Television made me cry, I hadn't
watched one in a year and it was full of beautiful sad women
why so sad? I thought again and again of the woodcutter,
when I knocked on his door and gave him twenty dollars
to clean the cabin I could not clean it. I can't, I said, but he
didn't move his hand, he didn't move at all. This man, you
understand, was like a statue, he hated me, my weakness,
and I threw the money—it was almost all I had—I threw
it at his chest. I couldn't meet his eyes. What color they
were. I wanted him to do it to me. Grab me or spit at me
or make love to me. But I think he just didn't care either
way. When you said goodbye it was you who could not even
stand. You kneeled at my feet. I said nothing. Didn't clutch
or scream. It happened to another body, the dead one, but
the woodcutter saw through that body, he cut to the quick.
He wouldn't pick up the money. I would have frozen except
for him. Could he have embraced me. Could he have said a
single kind word. I slid off the steps and he closed his door.

TICK

It was so hot in the cottage
when summer arrived

and my table
broke its leg, the cooler

kept leaking the ants
ate my legs inexplicably

drawn to the bed on the nights
I was alone, and I was

as in the beginning
alone. The woods

thickened. I knew the names
of the birds and the feeling of the mushrooms

smashed up against my bare back,
dirt

climbing the crack of my ass
as you rode me into the rock.

On the night
we said goodbye a tick

dug its head into my hip and you
dug it out

with a hot match and tweezers,
spreading the flesh with your hand while I stood wincing

at the mantel. For the first time:
you on your knees for me. I wondered why

there was no clock anywhere in the cottage. Why
no way to lock

the door. Why the woodcutter
never said it was his place, why I paid

rent to a woman with a post office box
and not to him across the path.

He
never spoke to me at all. The conspiracy

of men.

You made sure the head of the tick
wasn't hidden in a ridge

of cellulite. Blotted away the little dot of blood.
Put your tongue inside me

until I pushed your mouth away. You said
It's not the end

of everything.
You wiped your chin on the edge

of the blanket we left
on the floor where

you liked to fuck me from
behind. I looked at your watch. You better get going.

You folded my hands between your own. Don't do it like this.
You kissed each finger, still

on your knees.
How old you seemed, then.

And the woods
turning against me. You let the light

drain into the floor.
We could turn

to marble, I hoped. We could burn
all the way down

to the bones,
the black head of the spent match

curdled on the rug,
the whole room at last

fireless.

ONCE

Once upon a time—

the fox fingering his bride—
the dragon striking his tail on the stone—
the crow shitting in the stream—

Hail the goddamn god. You said.
The viper tensing beneath the leaf
her foot turning black in the grass

poof! That was the end of that.
She was dead before she knew it
the little pig letting you in.

Not just once
you dug your fists in her hair-folds
combing as you climbed—

you could have flown you could have crawled
or slithered belly-wise
but in the end it was a man's form you took

to take her in, right there on the cold floor
pushing past the silk
laughing into her neck.

She got a throatful whenever she opened her mouth.
She got iron she got lead she got done.
She wanted to rip right through you but it happened

every time the other way around. She couldn't learn
a new way to wear her hair a new
tower to sit in. She was a bit dumb.

It seemed like a good idea—
the only idea,
punching out the windowpane

so you wouldn't have to knock,
sleeping with her hair over the sill,
stripping the oak bare.

After you'd gone she'd think *ravished*,
good, she laughed and cracked
her knuckles splashed in the sheet

counted the marks on her arm.
The mirror told her she was beautiful
no matter how bruised how changed.

Once, you didn't appear for a whole evening and she
ate wax and almonds and smoked.
She was so wet by the time you arrived

you put your hand right through her.
So you are water now, too?

She thought she was everything!
You turned her over and over,
wondering at the parts of her that were wood,

that were born in the wild as you were born in the wild,
fur and gold and from the trees themselves
a black marriage.

In other words:
she lost it.
Her head hanging by a thread,

which the love-dogs snapped at day and night
the thread glistening, red
and delicious.

But the dogs
dragged back,
leaving dark dreams of wet teeth

and all her hair on the pillow
shocked clear of her scalp.
The mirror laughed.

She scooped up what was spilled
and hauled herself home,
heaving the skin suitcase

locked but leaking
a spoiled trail,
a bleak glistening in the dirt.

No one trod that path,
no tracker tracked.
You were long gone.

The sea intervened.
You tried to push your love across it simply
did not make it.

Stuck in some swell.
She could have done something different. Didn't.
Stumbled along.

Once free she spent a long time just wondering
what or where she was
touching the scar

on her neck the thread still fresh
howling for her lost nymphage
shaking the dead foot

trying to be human.
Knowing she must have been, once.
Cursing the feeling.

No beasts at all in the city
no bats no nothing
maybe some tanked fish in a Chinese restaurant that's it.

She sat outside with a piece of steak
waving it raw in the night—
Here, fox, she cried. *Here, dragon-dragon—*

cursed the tame things that came instead,
jabbed their ribs with her shoe
ate the steak and choked

wept steadily into a jar
licked the rim
cut her tongue

then went to bed and pissed it.

Pathetic!
She's not so pretty these days,
not nearly so prancing so proud—

I saw her in the glass and just had to laugh.
And her laugh was an echo, a leaf
pierced by the viper's teeth.

Sharpen those scissors.
Close the window.
Sing the fucking song.

I don't take gentleness for granted now
I don't let beauty in I just don't.

DEUS EX MACHINA

Drinking was one of the things I thought about doing. Because in the movies that's how it is, a beautiful drunk woman wandering around the city in a thin coat and high heels. But instead I was eating in bed all day listening to the traffic with the blinds closed I was so hungry I forgot what pens were for. Wore a single pair of stretch pants. Paid for the pizza in quarters. What was my a-ha moment you ask well I'll tell you. It was knocking a liter of Pepsi onto a stack of high school notebooks beside the bed I was shit-faced on Snickers and chicken wings that was my rock bottom. Seeing the paper bubble up brown, not even righting the bottle when I had the chance I cried with my mouth open and no sound coming out. What a fucking mess I'd made. At that time I thought mostly in curse words. What a fucking goddamn fucking fucked-up mess.

THE CUT

Without you to hurt me who will hurt me? Oh but you know
how, even a thousand miles away, you can do it: *I thought I
told you not to call me, never to call me here* and I hold the
phone beneath my cheek and dig just above the vein, calm
as clipped grass, and it's your hand, it's your hand

SICK

How was your trip my mother asks, holding a bag of
burritos; I have gained weight and she is thinking how to tell
me this and I just look at her I don't take the bag I don't say
your name and I don't say *Fine* I will never say your name
out loud again, not even to you, and though I don't know this
yet, how could I know it, I start to cry. I tell her it's about her
cancer, how I don't want her to die. She says *It's nothing, I'm
fine, I'll be okay, what is this? What is all this?* Meaning my
stained shirt and the dishes in the sink and the filth on the
floor and I say *cancer* when I mean *him* and we sit together
on the sofa, the food going cold, the brazen death-cells
tripling

INCANT

I forgot to say—there were not even electric lights. So light means something different now. When I got back to the city I wouldn't touch the switches. Dust grew thick on the bulbs I burrowed into the bedclothes broke my pencils ate erasers—

is it as simple as putting on clean underwear? Discarding the old doughnuts? Chopping new collarbones from the soft body of the caterpillar—choosing a new moisturizer?

I spent such a long time helping you find the best way to make me gag. Learning which plants wouldn't kill me a field guide propped beside the stove what mushroom to eat what spider to kill. I stare at a dish of venison trying to remember what the deer looked like tearing ivy from the trees I weep over a wedding present of expensive yellow sheets—

this is the ritual. Casting the sad spell. Drinking the old blood. It's you, every time, but less, and less.

PLAINS

I pulled over, hopping the old fence
and headed for the goats,

fruit against my chest
in the dress you said you loved.

I watched their mouths
chopping the apples:

chipped teeth pitting
the innocent

skins. Green. They must have been
sour, those apples, but they were

      eaten.

I kneeled in the dirt. The goats
closed in, lifting

my skirt. I looked into their strange eyes;
I wept into their filthy

furs. They let me.
When I rose to go

they followed. Braying faces.
Grass for miles. Corn

dying by the road.
We are not out

      yet.

REUNION

We don't speak for six months. You used to call me from an ancient pay phone, in the old days, but only to tell me some little thing—never where you were going, when you'd arrive. I dial that pay phone; it rings and rings. I imagine the sound slipping along the empty street, soaking into the floor of the wood, where the fox hears it, and the fawn, and the crow, keeping time. I imagine the incredible stupid deafness of the entire universe, how I wanted something, how I never got it, that pay phone nearly dead from disuse; I was keeping it alive, until I wasn't anymore.

When you do call I am better. *Well*, you say. *What's new?* There's a choice then, to breathe or not to breathe; I keep breathing. The sun in my eyes. I hear all the news. How you moved house. Towns. States. Countries. There's a drag on the line because of the distance. Everything is going well. For me, too, I say, and it's almost true. We laugh at the same time. I realize it's really you. And then I turn into an alley and put my hand up my skirt, my bag into a pool of thick milk. The skin is there, waiting for me to slip into it. Please dear god hit me, hit me. I'm sorry I thought I didn't want it. You want it? *No one does this.* No. No one. I fuse my ear to the phone. You have a class in five minutes, but you talk me through to the end. Ache in my wrist. We hang up and my hair is stuck to the brick and it's much deeper than I thought, this wound. How thin the scab was. How fat the maggot beneath.

AS TOLD BY ORPHEUS

So I turned back. They promised you were right behind but I know the sound of your step and you were definitely not stepping. Now I'm waiting to hear where they're going to send me. Not home. Not the earth, for sure, never again, that's what they said, though joke's on those motherfuckers: I don't like the world I don't like dancing or music or food I like you, even shadow even silent even quite gone from me harmony is overrated. I looked back and oh the lightlessness over my shoulder black on black velvet on pitch. Your name frozen between my teeth. That void. I held out as long as I could.

THE MAGICIAN

I met him outside. On a bench. I had been running. Had
stopped because I was breathing wrong, too hard, some
pain in my side, organ-deep, bladelike. He had been
running, too. Black suit. No sweat. Stopped to ask me
something. Behind me. Behind the bench. I didn't see him,
though there was a shadow, I remember, later, must have
noticed it later but not at first. The light behind me. A man
behind me. Even cramped up and airless I was thinking of
you, too full of this thinking to let anything inside. The holes
in me were not functioning, no eating for days, no blood for
weeks, and not speaking or shitting, nothing going in or
out, and I could not hear him, this other man, his shadow
thrown over my head like a hood, like something you put
on an animal, hawk or horse, to put a limit on its fear, its
possible fear, anticipating it, he laid his hand on me, on my
shoulder, while I was, as I said, listening to this thought of
you, endless thought, I was trying to get to the end of it,
and he touched my shoulder, he put his hand exactly where
you had put it, that time, behind me, behind me as he was
behind me, remember? That room? The smell of sage and
the tea steeping in the hot cups? And I made a sound, I cried
out, and he took his hand away, his shadow shifted, letting
some of the sun fall back on me, and I turned, the light in
my eyes and him so tall saying *Is this yours*, meaning the
headphones curled white in his palm, torn somehow from
my own ears; I hadn't noticed or known, I couldn't recall
music at all, hearing it or wanting it, he said he saw them
fall, and so they must be mine, and I was staring, I was
blinded, I was hurting where he had touched me, where you
had touched me, and he was waiting, he was expecting me
to speak, a man brought into the world where all men had
vanished and he kept standing there and I would have to,

I knew it, I would have to someday, soon, now, try to listen, again, to a man, another man, to make sense of him, of words, of a world in which a man could touch me, could bring me music, could insist on music, that it was mine, that I take it, that I look him in the eye, where there suddenly was that other star

THE VALLEY

I run every day   that's how I   lost   the weight.

You knew me   one hundred pounds   at the most

you cooked a steak I ate   the fried bit of fat and left

                the rest

I had bread for dinner and ripped berries from the stems even milk

                was

too   expensive then you   brought me

        red wine I   was

sick on it   so   never again

you put your hand around   my arm

        and the fingers met. When I left I ate

                                those frosted doughnuts

in the

thin plastic   sleeves and   cheap   meat swelled

fat as a tick.

Hunger a metaphor

for hunger.   And when I met   the   husband I
was

back to   nothing. Now I eat   like

my neighbors.

Look at this   suburb.   Big salads and

fresh   fish. I   don't gain. I don't   lose.

I keep the wine   down.

These little   black   dresses.

High heels.   Hair

sliced   to the   chin and dyed   light.

But you'd know me.

My hand still   trembles   on the   pen.

I still open my

eyes   when I come.

ECHO

I'll never get used to
seeing

house after house after house

the lawns
like dark jewels in the evening

between them. The way trees
stand shy so far apart

and the sky
halved of its stars—

Where are our stars? Our evenings? Our trees?
Good ghosts

tucked inside their mirrors,
haunting as quietly as they can.

IN MY DREAM
YOU CALLED ME ON A PHONE
MADE OF LEAVES
AND I ANSWERED

Hello?
It's me
Oh, you—
Who else?
No, no one.
Who else
You know I don't like the phone.
Who else
I meant to write
Who
I'm getting married
(wind)
I'm sorry
Who
I'm sorry I didn't call
Who
You don't know him
(wind)
You'd like him actually
(wind)
Are you still there
Mm
Are you mad
I'm thinking
Thinking what
Can't describe

Don't be jealous
Not, not
It's in May
(wind)
The wedding I mean
Do you love him
I don't know
You don't
Don't ask me
(leaves)
I've been sick
Shh
And so busy
Shh
And you didn't come
Not, not
We'll have pear trees
(wind)
In the spring
You don't
And music
Don't
Why didn't you
(leaves)
Just once
(leaves)
In the spring

NUDE

I kept making them, long after, you in between pages of
birds, of ferns, of bees; thick-thighed, adrift, the ink pressed
hard into the page, as if to pin you down: the way you sat on
the step, knees wide, cupping your chin as you listened; you
making tea at my stove; you sprawled before the fire, on a
blanket, facing the flames. I draw your back; it's what I can
stand to see. I buy men for class, to sit or stand or squat,
dicks dangling like wet socks on a clothesline, copied into
a dozen notebooks for me to nod at, yes and yes and yes, is
that how you see him? Is the light right? Where is his weight
on the page? When I draw a woman she looks tired, even if
she is twenty. There's no one to correct me, to say Just draw
the model. My husband sees the notebook on the table, flips
to your page, stops. I go quietly cold.

EXHIBITION

Exhibit A.
I was hanging a plant in my office when my husband came in
with salads. Surprise surprise, he said, and put the salads
down, put his hands on my hips. I said Oh no I'm working.
He said, Lunch break. I put my hands on my desk and stared
at the chair where students sit when they want to cry or yell
at me. Sometimes when someone is crying or yelling in that
chair I think about coming with my hand in a bed of spinach.

Exhibit B.
I showed up to my first class in a pink silk skirt. I taught
sitting down. When I stood, there were marks on the back
of the skirt, where my crotch had touched the fabric. I'd just
worn a thong and this is what I learned: No thongs. No silk.
No skirts.

Exhibit C.
It's a story from the Bible.

Exhibit D.
A male colleague sat next to me at a meeting and
complimented my work, which he said he'd seen in a show
downtown two years ago. So striking! I'm married, I said
right away, fingers curled over the edges of my notebook,
my wedding ring white beneath the fluorescent lights.
He laughed. Yes, he said, I *see*.

Exhibit E.
I spent my first paycheck on cocaine. I did all of it, stayed
up for twenty-six hours drawing piles of tentacles, which
I thought were brilliant and which are still actually quite
good.

Exhibit F.
F is for *You Fucked Up*.

Exhibit G.
I never get this far when hanging a show. I start putting the
work up randomly or else someone's curating anyway and I
leave it to them. You're supposed to put everything in some
kind of order. The men are very good at it. They take a long
time, saying Hm, no, not there, no, it doesn't *cohere*, no,
don't do it that way. In class I say it's so important, how you
present yourself. I pretend it's all on purpose. The run in
the stocking. The back of my head where I didn't quite
comb my hair.

DOUBLE

In class there's a girl who never takes
her big coat off.

She scratches at the paper with her pencil,
her marks so light

I have to squint to see them. She's drawn the model
as a bird. What are you doing here? I ask,

pointing at a wing. She shrugs. I've never heard
her speak. Her dark hair disappears into the neck

of her jacket and I almost touch it, how wild it is,
how it floats around her pale face

hiding her yellow eyes. We look at the model
together, the way his balls

hang between his legs. We look back at the board.
Her creature is sinking into the page

reluctant to show his treasure
even to us, who know him, who have seen

those treasures before.
She can't even hold a pencil

properly and I want to say
something cruel to her,

snap her out of whatever dream she's in.
There's a black bracelet around her wrist

from where a hand has held it. Who is this?
I ask. She shrugs. Please let me kill her.

How young she is, how pretty. I'll think of her
the next time I look in the mirror, the next time

you call. There's this girl, I'll say. And then
lose it. Can't

explain. Fury eating me from the knees up.

My husband comes to the show
and gives each student's work his kind eye.

The girl is there
in a chair by the door. Looking at her watch. About

to cry. Nails making moons
in her palms.

No one congratulates her
on her creature; you can't see him

from more than three feet away. Whoever she's waiting for
never arrives and she leaves

after an hour, face shattered, and doesn't
return. At the end of the semester I roll up her

work and put the tube in a closet
in case she comes for it. I call your office

again and again. I put on my winter coat
and don't take it off

when I draw. Making the lightest marks.
Holding the pen by the throat.

THE VIRGIN

I told it one night to a friend from school, her deep silence
in the studio, eyes fixed to mine. *Can you believe it*, I kept
saying. *Can you believe that I.* Our shoulders against the
stone wall I thought it would hurt her, a little, she who had
had no lovers, who had started the evening with pictures of
her sculptures and their great success, their themes global,
political, I was so eager to get her off them but she had tears
in her eyes, when I spoke, had I told it wrong? I went to the
desk, turned the old drawings over. Trailed off. She made
things out of iron, steel, enormous; a fire could not touch
her, nor a rip, nor a spill, and here I was, only paper, so easily
destroyed. I could feel her watching me, that silence of hers.
I had given away this thing and for the wrong reasons and
now could not take it back. *It's not like that*, I said, and she
put her hand on my sleeve. *Does he know?*

LONG DISTANCE

(quiet) (silverware) *What's your kitchen like.*

White.

Did you ever fuck in it?

Pardon?

Did a man. Fuck you in it. On the floor or against the stove or—

God, no.

(pause) *Good, then. That's good.*

There was something I wanted to tell you.

What, darling.

Forgot.

Today?

Yes, something I saw somewhere. Reminded me.

Of you or need to tell you something.

Tell me later. If you remember.

I will.

(pause) *I'm hard.*

(last plate)

What about you.

I'm going to wipe the counter.

(laugh) *But I want to fuck you.*

Well you can't.

No?

No.

(pause) *What's the matter.*

Nothing, it's—

What?

I'm holding this filthy sponge—

Well put it down, darling, Christ.

If we start we'll just have to stop.

There's time.

There's not.

Just for a moment.

I can't, let's just talk, I can't—
Please—
(pause)
All right.
(pause)
It doesn't matter.
(inhale)
Did you put the sponge down?
(small laugh) Yes.
Wipe your hands.
(wipes)
God, I can see you.
What do you see.
You with your elbows on the stove. The back view of you.
Bending for me.
(quiet)
I want to be inside you.
(sigh) (sorrow)
You're wet.
Yes.
Are you crying?
(wet exhale)
Because of the way I'm fucking you?
(quiet)
Let me hear you cry.
(swallow) (cries)
That's good. Good girl.
(pause) They're going to cut us off.
Darling.
And it's because—I just—
I know.
(whisper) It's such shit.

No, I know.
This is shit.
Listen, I'm there. I'm kissing your eyes.
Yes.
And—listen—
(listening)
The things I have said to you—
Yes?
—these things, they are yours, I have said them so—so few times—
(crumb on the floor) (very close to the floor)
—to anyone. You understand?
Yes.
Do you understand me?
Yes.
There is no one like you.
(quiet)
You know that. My dear. Don't you?
(crumb) (quiet)
I would kill—

QUEEN OF SWORDS

I sat with my mother on her birthday. All her hair had grown
back. She said You know I'm really proud of you I said why.
She said Well look at you so successful. She meant *thin*.
She loved my husband. I wanted to say Well look at you so
alive. Maybe that's what we mean, when we compliment
each other: Look at you, it hasn't killed you yet. Her hair
came back pure black. She looked unbelievably young. It
made her generous, this second beauty; she saw happiness
everywhere. I touched the red wool of the new couch.
Everything was red, now, she said she was tired of beige, the
tyranny of neutrals, it was all about strength and life and
love, wasn't it? Wasn't it, sweetheart?

THE HANGED MAN

It occurred to me, at the feast,
that we were spared:

you'd never seen me taking a shit,
or standing in line

at the post office.
I'd forgotten,

in the wood,
what life was like:
how full of painless things.
How huge.

I didn't have
blood or dew

to give. It did not make me new
to sit at the long table
hand heavy with gold.
Face fully made.

(You'd never even seen me in lipstick,
I thought, and is that sad? Or isn't it?)

I gave up everything I wanted

to have something else I wanted
more. I know why
you didn't think for a moment

of leaving her.
You spare yourself one fire
in order to endure

another.
Cooler. Eternal.

At the altar I was as calm as Joan
eyeing the pyre:

knees not shaking.
Cheeks as dry as chalk.

LINE

You call from the hospital hallway. Your oldest. The girl.
Skull fracture. Your voice is at its lowest, and I try not to
think about the other times I've heard it this way, hushed,
odd hours, splitting into a sigh, a laugh, a sob. Dear God.
I'm on the back porch looking at the enormous lawn. You
breathe on the line; I imagine the bleak thrill of it, me
holding your hand in that hallway. Pressing her hair back
from her head. Eating from a vending machine. I'm not
sure you even know it's me listening. Your head is in some
catastrophe loop. Car crash. No air bag and *Her face, her
face.* Shh, I say. I'm here. I can't help wondering: Who did
you call first? Me? Or the other one? How many others have
there been? I rub my eye, trying to scrub away the thought,
how stupid it is, after all this time, and especially now.
The lights go on behind me. He comes out to see who I'm
talking to, why there's no dinner on the table, but I don't
turn around. You and I silent, our heads on the pillow. Just
breathing. How long I've lived for that. Her chest beneath
the white sheet. You'll watch her sleep tonight and I, I will be
watching with you.

ENEMY II

We started out as usual. Me on the edge of the bed after a bath, soaked towel and medusa hair. My husband unstrapping his watch. What's wrong, he said. I didn't answer. Honey put on your pajamas. I don't want fucking pajamas! I yelled, flinching from his hand when he tried to steady me. Why do you keep doing that, he said. I put my face in my hands, a powerful gesture to a certain man, a man like my husband, who takes pity on things, whose pity leads him to love. Come on, you can tell me. So I told him Just this once. Please just the one time never again. I can't, he said, and I stroked his thigh Yes you can, spreading my knees, and when he said No again I slapped him—do you know what it's like, to see someone backed so thoroughly into a corner, wanting to come through for you, hating you?—and kept slapping until he put the pillow over my face, his fist through the feathers like he meant it, all wrong, and I reached for him, the both of us crying out, and that was when he wept, my beautiful husband, How could you make me? How could you? the pillow knocked away and him touching my face, touching it all over, shoulders shaking. I held him tight. How could you.

ACCOUNTING

There were   some   things   I stole   from you I   confess it

now   that you   are   gone now   that I am beyond the reach
                                                    of your long

eye   shall I   make   a list? Like   I did

when   I came   back   to the old   house   without you walking
                    the beaten

weeds

to the door when I   sat   on the cracked   step   dipping my finger
                    in spit

I heard Telemann   in my head   as I wrote   in the grit
                         on the porch plank

I heard you   tell me   how much your wife   loved you
                    as the mattress rolled

beneath   my cheek

I could count   all the times   with you   on a handful   of hands
                    and yet   it

seems there are years   crunched up   somewhere   in the space
                         between

weeks

and they have   aged me they have   worn me   smooth
      as lakestones

my knees so soft from kneeling   mouth   like moss
                           from sucking cunt

loosening

its little   beads   of blood

does it mean   something   your knuckles bridged

over my lips you were   tenderest   then   when we I was on   the
edge of

blacking

out.

About those things   I took:

I won't name them   just now. Maybe   not   ever.

I'll let you   test   your pockets   on your way   home the little
            doors

inside you.

I had all the keys. All except one.

CONSTELLATION

I'm trying to get it as pure as I can.
Exact in every movement. *This and this and this—*
you put me in my place. Even beneath you
I was among the stars, platinum, plasma,
set among your hips, gemlike, polished.
You were there, beside, Vulpecula and his goose
staining the north sky.

This is what I have to know now:
where to stow the crown. How to put by the sword.
How to staunch the flood that flows toward you.

I'm trying to get it as pure as I can.
I let the wood have its way; it was my way, too.

THE FAVORITE

I pay the old one well.
He accepts

checks, he spreads
the cheeks of his ass

if I ask, lifts his dick,
peels the foreskin

to show me the hole.

Today I want him
asleep. It takes

three minutes.

Head heavy on the back
of the chair the wood

dug deep against his lip,
gravity suckling

his tits. His robe
a silk ghost

on the lap of the carpet.

I get
my one hour, and then

he leaves, bow-legged,
without saying

goodbye. A woman will never know
the manners

of a whore, no matter
how much or how often

she pays.

The favorite snores.
I put up the ink.
I please

myself. The way his thigh
puddles on the seat,

a marble boat
on its sea

of crepe. To draw
is to drown.

He drools. *Dearest*,
I whisper,

It's time.

EMPRESS II

I rolled in the leaves spread my knees over a stone felt its
cold kiss through my jeans. Mouth open in the undergrowth,
beetle busy over my lip. I put my arms around the porch
post and kissed it, solemn, risking the frozen splinter, isn't
this what love is? Straddling the rotting trunk how grateful I
was to be made exactly thus. To cut my thigh on the branch.
To rub my cunt against the moss.

What was taken from you, I want to know. Or did you not
have what I had, so could not lose what I lost.

TRIPTYCH

It's one of those afternoons, private lessons, this time a
boy who is completely beautiful, his back a Bacon-esque
slab bent over the table, young and dark, and I'm sorting
through his pens when the mail comes, a letter, from you,
an excuse to slice your way into my head again, in case I'd
forgotten, the way you give your *t*'s sharp tails, I can only
read every other word, and you don't sign your name, and I
hear the boy's voice, a question—

—and I look at his easel and he says, I don't know what to do
here, touching some obscure moment in his drawing, I can't
even see what he means, and I stare with the letter pressed
against my hip, making a sound like I'm thinking, about his
problem, as if it matters, and at some point I feel his eyes
down my shirt, I haven't worn a bra, and I keep looking at
the paper. I'm older now, you write to me sometimes, you
don't call. I hand him an eraser without looking to see what
he thinks of my breasts, and he scrubs away the thing he
doesn't like, he makes new marks—

—while I sit by the window and cross my legs and refold
the letter and take up a pen and stake out in savage lines
the shape of this stupid talented boy, I don't care, I could sit
on his cock, I don't care, and I draw that, too, the crudest
fucking, the nib groaning against the page and he is looking
at me and I meet his eyes with so much fury he has to look
away and I close the book and toss it on a table and cap the
pen and then I just don't feel anything about any of it and he
finishes his drawing and I tell him to be more assertive and
then he gives me money and he leaves and I have to laugh
about it all, later, I don't keep your letter, I want to hurt you,
and this is the only way I know how.

CRONE

In her fifties
Tracey Emin married

a stone. She who had fucked
her way through every drawing

she ever made was now renouncing sex.
I had to look

at my own desk with some despair. Freud
brushed round and round

the breast. Balthus never stopped
painting the pubescent crotch.

In the novel you wrote about us
you never hit me; and when I asked you why,

you said in surprise
It was never about that.

Your work is all heart and mine—
mine is the wound.

Every marriage

is made of stone and like a stone
you sink, your home

is at the bottom. There was a space beneath the floor
in the cabin

full of roaches and I dropped a pen down there, once,
and had to feel for it

in the beetled dark made a wish became
a princess was saved by a steed and yet

here I am. The bottom. The stone. The garden, in spring,
a beautiful wedding.

DAPHNE II

He   moved   on. I could have   changed   back   shed the

leaves

       stepped free of the

bark gone on   my way but now   this   is my way.

In the   cool   green

      even the woodcutter   kneels.   Doesn't dare

      show me   his   saw.

I like to see the men   panting   heavy-eyed on their   horses

sniffing for   beauty as for   truffles   you can't carry it   off

without   destroying it   that's what I

would tell him   now   that's what I   meant, when the river

took me   from his

        arm.

And yet because he touched me   I am   this.

I see the sun   every day   after all

        how it hits me   in hours   all over

until the night   scrapes him   away   in layers   and I turn

        again   to silver

THE COLLECTOR

I took the girl's drawing and put it on a table near a closet.
How much, a man asked, how much?

It was not for sale. He touched the corner of the paper, said
It doesn't look like you. That's because

it's not, I replied, three walls of my newest drawings
dripping at my back. Star maps.

Fields. I knew him, a collector, who had bought
my first nude

fifteen years before.
He bent lower over the page.

These? you had said, shaken, when I showed you
    my notebook.
These are all me?

It's your pride
that haunts me,

my smile limp as I collected the compliments
of colleagues, one eye

on the door. The girl didn't show up.
Nor did the dragon.

The man would not move
from the table, as if

at the bedside of a dying
wife. I told him:

Just take it.
He hurried from the room

before I could change my mind,
the drawing

pinched beneath his thumb.
I was nowhere

and you
were nowhere

and I had given her away
and failed.

GIRL IN BLUE

What are you looking at now. Schiele, I say. Hip bones. Eye
sockets. Scribbled vulvas. Yuck, you say. No, it's beautiful.
Breasts? you ask, hopefully. Schiele didn't like breasts,
I reply, walking past the miserable haystacks, Monet's
sexless ponds. People stare. You're not supposed to be on
your phone in the museum. I eat a bowl of soup; you just
listen. What kind. Tomato. I spill some change on the patio.
Clumsy, you say, and I get hot in the face. Dusk. I stretch my
legs by the fountain, dip my sandals in, push the quarters
along the tile. Couples and their cutlery all around me. You
should have children. What? You don't explain. The phone
is going to go dead. I hold it tighter. This is costing you, I
say. Yes. A fortune. I'm going to Rome. We both think of it:
meeting there. The thought flexes its muscles, invincible for
a moment, then wastes, hobbling off through the minutes.
Have a wonderful time, you say. I will. We let the phone die. I
keep it pressed to my ear. The water circling my calves. The
fountain isn't for wading, someone tells me, and this seems
a great injustice, more than I can bear, to move from it. I
step out, my feet sliding in the wet leather. I make marks on
the marble all the way through the café to the last Schiele,
one I didn't describe to you, an old favorite: a little girl
holding closed the back of a blue dress. Her face in her arm.
A child. He went to prison for a while. Then he drew this.
She's in a different kind of prison. A security guard says,
Ma'am, we're closing. You'd say, Just a minute. She's still
looking. But I didn't want you to see her. To see me seeing
her. Ma'am. I close my eyes. Feel him at my back. I don't want
him to see my face. If he goes I'll go. But he doesn't. I have to
turn toward him. I keep my eyes closed, walk past, I feel his
surprise, how he steps sideways to let me pass. I know this
place like the back of my hand. Just follow the crumbs home.

RENAISSANCE

In the dream I look at so many paintings I have to lie across
the bed afterward, my eyes pulling out of their sockets, a
cold cloth on my forehead. Fresco painting fresco statuary
painting painting church painting. The men are relentless.
I go to Calabria, to the silver firs, and it's like being pierced
all over with little swords, I can't take a deep breath. Oh
my god, I say, oh my god oh my god, my fingers sliding over
my face. Everyone on the train is asleep. At the first stop
I get off, wanting to be lost, but the paths are everywhere,
turning me out with the tourists. I drink from a stream
and the water hisses in my throat, the taste of liquid rock,
it sinks right through me, sickening. In the hotel the foxes
come in through the window two at a time. Their tails
brushing my legs. I open them. A plate of fish wriggles in the
sink. I eat warm mozzarella by the handful, vomit into the
bowl. The foxes have a certain smell, I used to hate it, not
anymore. I hold them by their necks as they lick me. More
and more surround the bed, the bath, I go to wash and step
into a sea of fur, I wash the fox off with fox, the landlady
knocks, I don't answer, there's fox in my mouth, and the fish
is dry, and the paintings have followed me, the old masters,
stuck to the ceiling, they don't approve, they will kick me out
of the studio, I've taken too much vacation, I didn't light a
candle in the church, and I don't know how to paint and am
not going to learn now.

RUINS

Three girls scribble in notebooks next to me, anxious, they
feel it as much as I do—how dead this place is. Don't get
down on your knees, Calypso warns, headless, her stone
skirt cutting the water. You won't get up again.

HARUSPEX

It's in the   rotting. What woods do is die lightening   fire
   ash beetle

disaster   deep freeze. Departure. Then: the stirring
   beneath the leaves. Life plucking the future from
   its own sad gut.

Tityus knew:

every dusk a fresh feast. The swarm in the fallen trunk.

Tend   not the   wound

but the hunger: keep

                        eating. Tomorrow comes. And comes.

CROWN

Your hands on my throat,

the bruise lace
they left behind—

those crown jewels, that ghost

necklace.

PORTRAIT OF THE LOVER

The photographer proposes a show. Insisting, in his poor
English, that my bodies and his bodies are alike, turning his
pictures over like cards in a magic trick, slow, revealing boy
after boy in black and white, standing on one foot, smoking
cigarettes at the window, eyes full of contempt. When he
has laid them all out the photographer bows his head, hands
behind his back, and I can see, in the attitude of his lover,
that this is a habit with him, that he asks for mercy routinely.
I lean away in disgust. It's clear in the photos that the boy
doesn't want him, or not very much, and you, you wanted
me, we were absolutely united in that. No, I say, and he looks
at me as if he has some great secret. I have frightened you,
the photographer says, simply, distinctly, and gathers his
pictures, tapping the corners together. Later he will write
me: *The boy is died of AIDS*, has been dead for decades: I
understand, too late, the theme. Mourning. I am chilled,
when he leaves. I hold my hands over my eyes.

ALWAYS MY LYRES WILL HAVE YOU

You are in a video giving an interview   astonishingly old

      still   a full head   of hair

laughing   the   terrible   tremendous   arms

      I'd never seen   someone   age   so

muscularly so bitterly

So how is   *the underworld treating you* the interviewer

      asks   you say

It's missing   *one or two*   *things*   *otherwise*   *quite well*

      The women?

The women are fine   The children?   *Strong and*

grown

The dog?   *Dead*   *I'm afraid*   What about

      your book

What about   it   How much of it is   fiction   *All my books*

          are fiction

Well there's a rumor   *Hey fuck your rumor*   you smile, the

interviewer   smiles   it's your   kingdom

          after all

Can you read something for us   the interviewer   asks

Certainly you say crossing   uncrossing   your legs I

choke up

a cup of tea

your eyes beneath   the screen   on mine   you

                                                  sing

THE LOVERS

He likes a woman who breathes easy.
More and more I am that woman,

clawing through the belly of the wolf,
shredding its strong sides.

He slides the flesh from my nails
washes my wrists white.

There is love and then there is love.
His kind sticks but leaves no stain. Its pleasure

is smooth, pitless. I needed a subtler skin for it,
a quieter mind—so I got them. Cell by cell.

Shedding the old ways.
I made a candle a candle, a tree

a tree.
I uncut you from water,

from stone, from leaves.
No more stars. No more sky.

Nature very silent now.
The wood quiet and fragile as eggs,

inside, untouched.
There are things he knows

watching my back at the window,
as I watched yours, years before:

deep night,
not letting me go.

HOSPICE

Unlike her father I was careful to die in front of her.
She was reading a book; I waited.
Then she lifted her head.
Mama! she cried.
Only then did I step through the door.

WEEDS

I wouldn't say
her death organized me.

Only that there are deaths
and there is Death.

I had a difficult time
approaching my notebooks

without thinking of sheets, shrouds,
how light she lay

on a blank page.
Paper seemed complete as it was.

You knew it was coming?

you said. Oh yes, I knew.
It was very calm, how it happened

and I felt how death could be a friend,
how it was separate from dying,

the true monster.
Anyway

I'm cleaner now, I said. Not knowing what it meant
but it was true. The pressing feeling

wasn't so bad anymore.
I'd said to her

There was a man, once.
She scraped her Jell-O.

I put my face in my hands.
You don't have to tell me, she said.

So I didn't. I just opened the book
and showed her your picture

on the flap of the jacket. She smiled.
Very handsome, she offered,

and closed her eyes. I went on
looking at the book

thinking *It's over.* And I knew it,
a little at a time,

as her urine drew a cold circle
beneath her yellow hips.

THE TOWER

Peace is blue, isn't it. Prussian. Almost black. I have jars
   and jars of it.

A shadow at the door, and then the light—

your face. Calm, just the way it was when we met.

Knowing something, about yourself, about me—

was it dread?

Or joy?

A step into a house built to fall, a house

already burning.

I never pleaded to undo

what was already done—

is it done?

I pour the ink on the page.

That blue.

It lasts.

Author photograph by Lewis McVey

MARYSE MEIJER is the author of *Heartbreaker*. She lives in Chicago.